#2

LOST IN SPACE™

THE NEW JOURNEYS

The Passengers

NANCY KRULIK

SCHOLASTIC INC.
New York Toronto London Auckland Sydney

ISBN 0-590-18939-5

12 11 10 9 8 7 6 5 4 3 2 1   8 9/9 0 1 2 3/0

Printed in the U.S.A.

First Scholastic printing, July 1998

For my parents, Gladys and Stephen Krulik,
who always encourage me to reach for the stars.

The Passengers

1
Battle of the Space Captives

"Checkmate!" The Robot triumphantly announced his victory. The lights in his clear bubble-shaped head flashed on and off while the knobs on his control panel clicked excitedly. His head whirled around a few times before he crowed, "That's three games to one, Will Robinson. Too bad for you."

Will, the Robot's ten-year-old opponent, looked at the chessboard and shook his blond head. "Show-off! Remember, nobody likes a bad winner. Remind me to program some modesty into you the next time you have a tune-up."

Will looked at the three-dimensional holographic chessboard and scratched his head. That was the third time this week that the Robot had beaten him in chess. And to think that Will was the one who had programmed the Robot to play chess in the first place! He had obviously programmed him a bit too well. Now Will had two choices — he could either reprogram the Robot, or learn to play a better game of chess.

Will opted for perfecting his chess game. Quickly he reset the holographic pieces on the multilevel video chessboard. "I'll

1

get you this time!" Will told the Robot as he clicked onto a black pawn and contemplated his opening move.

But Will's concentration was broken when his fourteen-year-old sister Penny wandered into the room. As usual, Penny was dictating her journal into her tiny wrist video recorder. Will thought Penny's journal was the most boring collection of thoughts ever assembled in the universe. But Penny was certain that the diary, which she referred to as *The Video Journals of Penny Robinson, Space Captive*, would someday be devoured by millions of readers, and that she would become a celebrity throughout the galaxy.

"The Young Space Captive moved through the lonely ship, staring out into the never-ending night," Penny proclaimed. "She thought about her friends back on Earth. They might have gathered at one of their houses to do some virtual shopping. Holographs of models in the latest fashions would be flooding the room they were in, and the girls would be keying their orders into their pocket computers. Later they might put on their jet-packs and whiz over to the pizza parlor, hoping to share a slice with some of the new recruits from the Academy. The Young Space Captive had to wonder: Was a boy there waiting for her, dreaming of her? A boy with his own sports flight vehicle — a romantic two-seater? Of course, the Young Space Captive was not allowed to go on vehicle dates yet, but that didn't really matter, because she was lost in space with her family, with no hope of reaching home anytime soon." Penny ended her tirade with a loud sigh. She ran her fingers through her shaggy dark hair and shook her head.

Will tried so hard to hold back his laughter that a loud snort burst through his lips. Will hated when Penny called herself "the Young Space Captive." She was so dramatic.

Still, Will shared Penny's longing for the things back home.

2

He knew that Tommy Wolden had probably taken his short-stop position on the Little League team. And by now, most of the other kids would have finished their unit on mid-twenty-first-century transportation and received their transporter licenses. They'd be able to pop from class to class while Will would still be walking like all the little kids.

But most important, Will knew he would miss winning the next school science fair. Will was a real science brain. When it came to competitions, the other kids never stood a chance against him. Will frowned. The other kids were probably glad he wouldn't be around for the science fair.

Will figured that the chances were pretty good that he would never even participate in another school science fair. He'd be lucky if he ever saw another kid again. After all, the Robinsons had been floating around in space on board the *Jupiter 2* for more than a month now. And they still had no idea where they were, or how to get back to Earth.

When Will's dad, famous research scientist John Robinson, first announced the family's journey on the *Jupiter 2*, Will had really been excited. Who wouldn't have been? The Robinsons had been chosen to be the first settlers on Alpha Prime, a planet upon which water and food would be in endless supply. Will's family was going to pave the way for Earthlings to start over on this new paradise, to show them how to live without depleting natural resources. The Robinsons were going to save the world.

At least that was how it was supposed to be. These days the Robinsons were lucky if they could save themselves from the hideous monsters, blinding meteor storms, and treacherous black holes that they encountered as they floated blindly through space.

Had the mission gone as planned, Will, Penny, their older

3

sister, Judy, and their parents, John and Maureen, would now all be comfortably tucked away in their cryogenic sleep pods, safely dozing their way to Alpha Prime. Their bodies were supposed to have been frozen into a deep sleep that was meant to last for ten years — the time it would take to get from Earth to Alpha Prime.

But the mission had gone horribly wrong — and now here they were, along with their pilot, Major Don West, and a villanous stowaway, Dr. Zachary Smith, trapped in an alien galaxy far from home. At least Will thought they were far from home. There was no way of telling just how far from Earth they really were. The stars were all arranged in new and unfamiliar constellations, and traditional navigational experience and equipment served no purpose.

Will's thoughts were interrupted by another of Penny's mindless musings into her video recorder.

"Would the Young Space Captive ever feel the touch of her first real kiss?"

"Well, I could program Robot here to kiss you, Pen," Will remarked sarcastically.

The lights in Robot's head flashed suddenly. He turned away from the holographic chessboard and rolled quickly toward the door.

"Where are you going?" Will asked Robot. "We have a rematch to play."

"I am off to find some ice cream. That is something I am programmed to enjoy. But I am not programmed for such public displays of affection as kissing, Will Robinson."

Will laughed. "Relax, buddy. No one is going to kiss you. I wouldn't be that cruel to an innocent robot!"

The Robot's lights flashed again as he ran a quick check of his vocabulary memory bank. "Kissing as a display of cruelty does not compute, Will Robinson. Kissing is about affection and love."

"Believe me, Robot, kissing Young Space Captive here would be unnecessary cruelty. A violation of the space code of ethics."

Penny flicked off her recorder and scowled. "Very funny, galaxy geek." She looked at Will and his Robot and laughed. "Look at you, Will, playing with your big metal dolly. You are such a child!"

Now Will was mad. A child? He was only four years younger than Penny. And how dare Penny call the Robot a doll! Robot was a sophisticated mass of wires and computer chips. He was smarter than Penny, and he could carry on a much more interesting conversation with Will than she could.

"At least I have someone to talk to all day. I don't spend my time talking into a video camera like you, Space Craptive." Will grabbed the recorder from his sister, rewound the tape a bit and pushed play. Penny's voice filled the room. "Don West thinks of me as a child, but I am so much more than that."

"Ooooh, Don, you cutie." Will made his voice high and squeaky as he imitated his sister.

"Give that back to me, you creep!" Penny ordered, grabbing for it. Her cheeks burned red as her secret crush was broadcast for everyone to hear.

"Come and get it!" Will dared her. He leaped up onto a table and held the watch/video cam high above his head.

Penny pulled the plug on Will's holographic chess game and leaped up on the table beside him. "Don't you push me, Will Robinson," she threatened.

"Hey, good idea, sis." Will reached out and gave Penny a tiny push. She fell to the floor with a thud.

"What is going on in here?" their mother's voice exclaimed.

"Will stole my video journal," Penny complained.

"She called Robot a doll," Will countered. "And she destroyed our chess game."

"I'll destroy more than that if you don't give that back to me," Penny told him. She lunged toward her brother once again.

Maureen Robinson situated herself between her two feuding offspring. "You two had better learn to get along," she said sternly. "We're not having any other company anytime soon."

Slowly, Will handed the video watch back to Penny. Penny hung her head low, twirled her shoulder-length dark hair around her forefinger, and muttered a semi-sincere, "Sorry, Will."

Maureen smiled. "That's better. I think you two have far too much time on your hands. And I can take care of that. I want both of you up on the bridge for a life sciences lesson in five minutes."

Will and Penny groaned in unison. Not more lessons! They both had figured that the one good thing about being lost in space was that they wouldn't have to go to school or do any homework. But they had been wrong. Their mom had taken over their schooling. And she was tougher than any teacher they'd had back on Earth.

"Think of it this way," Maureen commented. "You'll be all caught up with your schoolwork when we get back to Earth."

"You mean *if* we get back to Earth," Penny sullenly corrected her.

"No, I mean when," Maureen replied. But her voice didn't sound convincing.

2
The Noise

Penny and Will took their seats at the main console of the *Jupiter 2*. Major Don West and their older sister, Judy, were busy at the helm, programming the ship's main computer bank to accommodate the family's approximated weight and oxygen intake. Will watched as Major West leaned over and brushed a wisp of Judy's blonde hair off her face. He was pretty sure Penny had seen it, too. Will kicked Penny under the table. Penny blushed red.

"Cut it out, Will," Penny hissed.

"Today, let's take a look at the use of DNA manipulation in cloning procedures," their mother interrupted before Will and Penny could get into another argument.

"She sounds just like a teacher," Will whispered to Penny.

"I hear just like a teacher, too," Maureen told Will. "For the next few minutes just pretend I am your teacher, okay?"

"Boy, this is all the hard parts of school without any of the fun," Penny moaned.

Mrs. Robinson ignored Penny's complaint. She was used to her daughter's theatrics. She turned on one of her computers and a picture of a long brown worm filled the screen.

"Worm DNA is simpler than human," she began.

"Why are we studying worms, Mom?" Will asked. "We're not likely to encounter any of them out here in space, are we?"

"You never know what kinds of creatures we may encounter," his mother explained.

Just then, a tall, thin man with a light brown goatee barged angrily onto the bridge. Behind him, a monkeylike creature, the size of a chimpanzee, bounced up and down. The creature had spiny yellow skin, dragonlike scales, and bright blue cat's eyes.

"Hey, Will," Major West called over from the console. "See, your mom was right. Here comes a worm right now."

Dr. Smith ignored Major West's comment. He pulled angrily at his goatee and glared at Penny. "Will you keep this creature out of my quarters, please," he demanded. "Otherwise, I might be tempted to make a belt out of its lizardlike skin!"

The creature leaped over to Penny's shoulder and clung tightly.

"Blawp. Blawp," the creature purred.

"Hey there, Blawp," Penny said, gently stroking the pet's skin. Blawp's skin color changed gradually until it blended in with Penny's red space suit. Penny kissed the creature on the nose. "Do you want to study DNA, too?" she asked.

"Blawp. Blawp," Blawp replied.

Penny laughed and gave Blawp a big hug. As far as she was concerned, Blawp was the only good thing about being stuck on board the *Jupiter 2*. Judy had brought the creature back from an expedition she had taken onto an alien spaceship. She had said Penny could keep Blawp as long as Penny promised to take good care of her. So far, Penny had kept her word.

"You can stay with me," Penny told Blawp.

Blawp curled up in Penny's lap like a baby. Then she glared angrily at Dr. Smith.

After the interruption, Penny and Will settled in for their lesson. Will was exceptionally excited by the computer program his mother had chosen. He had been considering doing a cloning project for his next science fair when they were back on Earth.

Penny, however, was not as excited as Will. She didn't share her parents' love of science the way he did. As far as Penny was concerned, science was okay, but it was really literature and history that she adored. Still, today's lesson was science. Penny opened up her laptop laser notebook and began creating a genetic chart for a cloned animal. As she thought, she tapped her laser writing utensil (or LWU as it was called) on her notebook. It was an irregular beat, at first fast, then slow, then triple time. It took Penny awhile to realize that she was tapping to a beat that was coming from the transmission console.

"Hey, what's that banging?" Penny asked.

Major West went over to the console. "I'm not sure," he said. "I've never heard it before." Major West pushed a few buttons, testing for malfunctions. There were none. At least none that he could identify.

Quickly, Major West paged Professor Robinson. Will and Penny's dad rushed onto the bridge.

"We're having some sort of unidentifiable malfunction," Major West told the professor.

The adults (other than Dr. Smith, who never helped with anything) sprang into action. One by one they reviewed their stations, checking out equipment and supplies. Judy made certain that the oxygen and water supplies had not been affected.

Professor and Dr. Robinson checked the newly restored navigational computers. Major West checked all defense and steering systems. They could find no malfunctions.

But this discovery did not please the adults. Had they found the problem, they would have gone to work quickly to adjust it. But a mystery aboard the ship could be dangerous. There was always a chance that something major had gone wrong, and that the crew of the *Jupiter 2* did not have the equipment with which to fix it. Had they been in contact with Earth, someone in Mission Control could have run a ground check to tell them what was wrong. But with no way of contacting Control for advice, the crew of the *Jupiter 2* was on its own.

Major West set the ship on autopilot and prepared to make a space walk. If the malfunction wasn't inside the ship, perhaps it was outside.

"Be careful out there, Major," Judy said quietly as she helped Don adjust his breathing apparatus. "This isn't the space atmosphere you've trained under. It's almost impossible to predict the force of the gravitational pull of the closest star."

Don grinned. "Don't worry, Doc. The pull on me here is definitely stronger." He placed the helmet on his head and gave Judy a wink. Then he stepped into the exit hatch and prepared to leave the ship.

3
Talking in Code

Will remained uncharacteristically quiet as Major West prepared for his space walk. He listened carefully to the beat, pulled out his LWU, and began scribbling in his notebook.

"How can you think about doing your gene chart at a time like this?" Penny asked her brother. "We could be in grave danger. What if it's the oxygen system that's failing? We could all suffocate. Or what if one of our heat-conducting shields has burned out? We could all freeze to death."

Will ignored his sister and kept on writing. Finally, he looked up. "I think you can cancel that space walk, Major," he said confidently. "I don't think the clicking noise is coming from a malfunction. It's a code. Someone, or something, is trying to get in touch with us."

Major West stared at Will in disbelief. He had been almost out in space by the time Will stopped him. "Nothing like waiting for the last minute, Will," he replied irritably.

"Well, I wasn't sure at first," Will explained. "But now I'm pretty certain we're getting a message from another ship."

"That's impossible," Dr. Smith interjected. "There's no one

around here for light-years. Certainly no one who could have the capability of transmitting messages in any sort of code that a mere boy could understand."

"Go ahead, Will," Professor Robinson urged, ignoring Dr. Smith's ranting. "Let's hear your hypothesis."

Will smiled proudly. Back on Earth, his father had been too busy to even come to Will's school science fairs. But here in space, Professor Robinson considered Will a valued member of his crew.

"Well, the code itself is kind of crude, but it sounds like one used in the late twentieth century by members of certain space station communities to contact their shuttle personnel. So far, all I can make out are a few words. But they're important words." Will pulled out his notebook and read from his notes. "'We need help. Ship in trouble.'"

"The code is in English!" Penny shouted excitedly. "You mean there are humans nearby?"

"Now, don't get excited, Pen," Judy warned her younger sister. "After all, the people or creatures who sent that message could have sent it years ago, and it only reached us now. We have no idea how many light-years away they are ... or were."

"No, I think Penny's right, Judy," Don West said with excitement building in his voice. He turned some knobs on top of the main computer console. "The computer is now registering some form of electrical energy on the screen. Someone, or something, is out there. And they are not very far away."

Penny's mind began to race. "Dad, is it possible that we've drifted back into our own galaxy without even knowing it? You said that was possible, didn't you? I mean, maybe it's a rescue ship or something. Maybe people in our solar system are still searching for us. Maybe they know we're still alive!"

"No, honey, we're nowhere near Earth, much as I wish I could say we were," John Robinson gently told his daughter. "None of these constellations is familiar, and according to our navigational readings, the solar energy waves from the nearest star are nowhere near as powerful as those from our sun. I'm not sure what kind of life-form is on board that ship out there, or even where they are from. But I don't think they could be from Earth."

"But anything is possible, isn't it?" Penny insisted. "And if they're not from Earth, how come they know our communication codes?"

Professor Robinson had no answer for that one. Penny smiled triumphantly.

"Well, whoever they are, they're in big trouble," Will declared. "They're trying to tell us that their ship is refusing to function. If we don't find them fast, whoever is sending that message is liable to travel way off course."

"Oh, Daddy, we can't let that happen!" Penny said. "We've got to help them."

"Can you pinpoint their location, Don?" Professor Robinson asked.

"Excuse me?" Dr. Smith interjected. "Don't tell me you're actually considering looking for this so-called spaceship."

"What are we supposed to do, ignore them?" Penny shouted angrily.

"Exactly, Penny precious," Dr. Smith replied. "Ignore them at all cost. Who knows what kinds of aliens are out here? Doesn't anyone remember those horrible spiderlike creatures that almost killed us all?"

Will nodded. He remembered those aliens all right. It was hard to forget the giant spiders who had invaded Dr. Smith's body, threatening to turn him into one of their own.

Dr. Smith noted the disgust on Will's face. "Obviously the boy knows what I mean. Aliens cannot be trusted. They are all evil."

"BLAWWWWP!" Blawp squawked loudly in protest of Dr. Smith's words.

"You tell him, Blawp," Don West said with a grin. "Frankly, Smith, if anyone around here is evil, it's you, not some alien."

"Why, you barely evolved gorilla, how dare you speak to me like that!" Dr. Smith retorted.

Professor Robinson placed one hand on Dr. Smith's shoulder. "Calm down, Doctor. I can honestly tell you I am not considering going in search of that ship —" Professor Robinson began.

"Well, good," Dr. Smith interrupted. "At least someone around here has some sense."

"I'm not considering it," Professor Robinson continued, "because I've already decided. We will search for this ship and attempt to rescue anyone or anything that is on board. The purpose of this mission has always been to save lives, not to allow them to be destroyed."

Professor Robinson ignored the doctor's angry gaze and returned his attention to his son. "Will, I don't recognize this code at all but . . ."

"That's because it was never used much. I only learned about it last semester while I was researching a science project on early space communication," Will explained.

Penny groaned. Her brother could be such a show-off.

"Are you fluent enough in this code to be able to transmit a message?" Will's father asked.

"I can tap out the beat, Dad, but I don't know if I can transmit it at the same time."

Penny jumped to attention. "That's no problem, Dad. I can

do it. Will, you tap out the beat, and I'll repeat it. Between us, we'll get a message to that ship."

Will reached over and gave his sister a high five. Deep down, he really liked it when he and Penny were on the same side.

"Okay, Dad, what do you want me to tell them?" Will said.

"Let them know that we are unable to give them our exact location because we are unfamiliar with this universe. We will come to them if they can release a force field from their ship which can be recognized by our computers. It's the only way we can find them."

Dutifully, Will used his LWU to tap out his father's words on the table. Penny listened carefully and repeated each of the taps in the proper rhythm. The message seemed to be taking forever to transmit, but in reality the whole process took only about a minute and a half.

Will wiped a bead of nervous perspiration from his brow as he listened to Penny tap out the last of the clicks. He was pretty certain that he and Penny had transmitted their father's message correctly, but they had no way of knowing if the other ship was capable of receiving it, or if the ship had the capability of sending out a force field strong enough to be recognized by the *Jupiter 2*'s computers.

There was nothing they could do but wait.

4
The Big Gamble

Penny sat beside the transmission console, turning the volume dials higher and higher. The tapped-out code still seemed to be coming from the other ship, but the sound had become fainter, almost inaudible. And then the tapping stopped completely.

Penny frantically retyped the message she had most recently sent. She waited anxiously for the response. None came. "We've lost contact with them, Dad," Penny said, trying hard not to let her disappointment show.

"Do you think they've drifted out of our range, John?" Maureen asked her husband anxiously.

"I have no idea," Professor Robinson replied thoughtfully.

"Well, I say good riddance," Dr. Smith said. "You people take far too many chances. Now I think I'll go back to my quarters and relax. This has been an extremely stressful afternoon."

"And it's about to get more stressful, Smith," Major West remarked. He pointed to a small blinking light that had appeared on the *Jupiter 2*'s main computer screen. "That sure looks like a force field to me. Congratulations, kids, it looks as

16

though they not only received your message, but they understood it completely."

Will could hardly contain himself. He leaped up in the air and raised his fist high. "All right!" he shouted. Then he blushed and sat quietly in his seat the way a cool, calm, and collected officer on an important space mission should.

Professor Robinson walked over and wrapped his arms around his two youngest children. "I'm really proud of you two. You really worked together as a team. You are fine crew members. And thanks to your actions, hundreds of lives may just have been saved."

"This whole space journey is turning into one awesome field trip!" Will exclaimed.

"That's one way of looking at it," his mother said with a laugh. She gave him a quick peck on the cheek. Will was so excited about his father's praise — and the possibility of meeting up with other humans — that he forgot to be embarrassed by his mother's public display of affection.

"Well, this adventure isn't over yet," Judy reminded everyone. "We still have to reach that ship before it steers off course or . . ."

Judy didn't finish the sentence. She didn't need to. Everyone on board the *Jupiter 2* knew what she meant. The responsibility for the lives of everyone aboard that spaceship was in their hands.

Major West immediately got to work reprogramming the ship's direction. With Robot's assistance he was able to calculate the distance between the *Jupiter 2* and the ship that had just given off the force field. The two ships were not as close as he had hoped. "We're going to have to make this baby move if we want to reach them in time," he explained as he prepared the speed settings on the *Jupiter 2*'s main computer.

The Robinsons took their flight positions. Will and Robot kept an eye on the navigational controls. Penny stayed at the transmission console. Maureen watched the life-support indicators for any sudden drops in oxygen levels, while Professor Robinson and Major West took control of the helm. Dr. Smith, as usual, sat by himself, sulking in silence.

"Prepare to increase speed," Major West warned the others.

Professor Robinson checked to make sure his family was safely harnessed in position. Then he nodded to Major West. "Ready to engage," he said.

The crew of the *Jupiter 2* lurched forward as the ship suddenly increased its speed. But after that initial blast of energy, the ride turned smooth. Penny stared out the viewscreen while she hummed a tune that had been a huge hit the day they left Earth. Will joined in on the chorus. For a while, it almost seemed as though the Robinsons were on a carefree car trip to the beach.

SLAM! The merriment was suddenly interrupted by a powerful strike along the right side of the *Jupiter 2*. The giant ship was sent reeling to the left.

"What was that?" Dr. Smith asked.

"Darn it!" Major West exclaimed.

"I don't like the sound of that, Don," Judy said. "What's going on?"

The major gritted his teeth. "Meteor storm," he said. "A big one."

"I don't mean to say I told you so," Dr. Smith began. "But once again, I am . . ."

"If you say 'I told you so' one more time, Smith, I'll string you out there in space and let you catch the meteors in your big mouth!" Major West barked.

Professor Robinson focused the major's attention back on the problem at hand. "Can we take it, Don?" he asked. "Or do we have to turn back?"

Will felt his stomach churn. Turn back? How could they turn back? There were people out there who needed their help. But if they didn't turn back, the meteor storm might damage the *Jupiter 2* irreparably. And then they would be the ones in need of help. Will waited anxiously to hear Major West's assessment of the situation.

Major West was not one to avoid a little danger. In fact, he thrived on adventure and excitement. "Oh, we can take it all right," he said as he transferred the ship's steering mechanisms to manual control. "Hang on, folks. We're in for a bumpy ride."

Major West wasn't kidding. The meteors were coming at the ship from all angles, lighting up the sky like hundreds of red-hot flares. The rocks bashed into one another, causing fiery explosions through the dark sky. Major West steered the *Jupiter 2* at an almost impossible speed, dodging the burning rocks at every turn. He knew he couldn't avoid all of the rocks, so he tried to keep from colliding with the largest ones. Smaller meteors smashed the *Jupiter*'s outer hull, causing the ship to rock wildly from side to side. It felt as though the ship was going to career out of control at any minute. Will couldn't help thinking that if this had been a ride at an amusement park, he'd be having a blast right now. But this was real. Too real!

Suddenly, two huge meteors headed right for the *Jupiter 2*. It would be almost impossible for Major West to avoid hitting at least one of them.

Most men would have been panicking by now. But Don West was used to tight squeezes. He pushed a few control levers up as high as they could go. The *Jupiter 2* lunged forward, speeding directly for the space between the two huge stones. Then, with a sudden burst of motion, the spaceship leaped over the meteors, like a whale breaching in the ocean.

But the ship couldn't move fast enough to clear the meteors entirely. The one to the left of the ship clipped the *Jupiter 2*'s tail with a force so powerful it threw Dr. Smith from his chair. He slammed his head on the corner of the console. Unlike the Robinsons, Dr. Smith had not buckled into a harness.

"Oooow," he moaned. "Now see what you've done, West."

But nobody heard the rest of Dr. Smith's ramblings. His words were blocked out by the sound of a huge explosion behind the *Jupiter*. The pressure caused by the ship's collision with the meteor had sent the giant rock swirling in a different direction. It smashed head-on into the other meteor. The two giant rocks exploded in a huge display of fireworks.

The danger wasn't over yet. Another sea of meteors lay ahead. But these were smaller rocks, easier for Major West to avoid. He swerved the ship back and forth, avoiding the meteors as though they were traffic cones on a highway.

And then the meteor storm ended, just as abruptly as it had begun.

At first, no one said a word. They all sat quietly, contemplating what they had just been through. Finally, Major West broke the silence.

"Our next fireworks show will be in fifteen minutes," he joked. He seemed calm, but Will noticed his hands were trembling.

"Will and Penny," Professor Robinson said, snapping into action, "see if you can contact the other ship again. Let them know we're still on the way."

"Yes, sir!" Will said with a salute. Quickly, he used his LWU to tap out the message on the console table. Once again Penny echoed his sounds while sending out the transmission.

Then, just as earlier, the crew of the *Jupiter 2* awaited a reply. But this time, no response came. "You don't think we were pushed off course during the meteor storm, do you?" Penny asked Major West.

"No, Penny," Major West said. "We're still headed in the right direction." Penny's face fell. "Maybe they've received the message, but no longer have the energy supply that they need to transmit a response from their ship," he suggested.

Penny brightened slightly. Major West had a good point.

Will looked out into the dark sky, searching for some sign of the ship. He saw a blinding flash of light, followed by a massive explosion.

"Not another meteor storm!" Will cried out.

Professor Robinson shook his head. "No, Will. I have a feeling that explosion was something much worse."

"Oh no!" Penny shouted. "You don't think that was the other ship, do you, Dad?"

Don West's face grew grave. He nodded quietly and pointed to a computer reading of the makeup of the atmosphere surrounding the other ship. It showed increased radiation distortions — a sure sign that the ship had broken up.

Penny felt her heart sink. In a strange way she had already developed a bond with the people on the other ship. And now they were gone. Forever.

For awhile, no one said a word. Then Dr. Smith stood and rubbed his head angrily. "So this was all in vain, eh. Here I am injured, and there aren't even any aliens left to rescue. Honestly, the danger you people put me in . . ."

"Guess you took on more than you bargained for when you agreed to kill us all," Major West said.

Will watched Dr. Smith's reaction closely. No way could he argue with that. Dr. Smith had tried to kill them right at the beginning of their mission.

Before Dr. Smith could reply, Judy interrupted. "Don, do you see something odd out there?" she asked.

"Odder than usual?" Major West asked with a grin.

"Yes. Over there to the left. It seems to be some sort of metal object."

Maureen moved closer to her eldest daughter. "It could be a piece of the other ship," she offered.

"I don't think so, Mom," Judy said. "It appears to be moving in a very definite direction. It seems to be coming toward us."

Will's mind flashed to the *Jupiter 2*'s remote probe ships, small vehicles attached to the main ship. Maybe someone from the destroyed spaceship had managed to get away in time on board a remote vehicle.

"I think someone's escaped!" Will declared.

"That's absolutely ridiculous," Dr. Smith interjected, once again dismissing Will's ideas.

"Not at all, Doctor," Professor Robinson declared. "Penny, Will, try to regain contact, but this time with that remote vehicle."

Penny reprogrammed the computer's transmission device to match the direction and speed of the remote vehicle. Then she and Will began the tap-tap-tap process once again.

There was no response. But the vehicle did appear to continue moving toward the *Jupiter 2*.

"Either the people on board don't know how to use the transmission devices, or they are injured too badly to use them," Judy hypothesized. "Either way, we're going to have to get on board that ship and help them."

Dr. Smith was about to return to his cabin.

"Not so fast, Smith," Judy called out. "I'll need your help when we board that ship. We have no idea how many people are on board, or what condition they are in. I'll need all the medical assistance I can get."

"There's no way I'm going on board that ship," Dr. Smith replied defiantly.

Professor Robinson and Major West stood threateningly on either side of Dr. Smith. "I think you will be going on board, Smith," Professor Robinson declared. "You took an oath to help sick and injured people, you know."

"People, yes. Aliens, no," Dr. Smith argued.

"Well, until we have evidence to the contrary, we have to assume those are people," the professor said. "Prepare to board the probe vehicle."

Judy and Don accompanied the doctor to the lower deck. John Robinson turned and spoke to his wife and two younger children. "Maureen, keep an eye on the radar from the probe. Keep track of our every move."

"I always do." Maureen smiled.

"Will and Penny, keep trying to contact that vehicle. Even if they can't reply, maybe they can receive transmissions," Professor Robinson directed.

"Dad, take Robot with you," Will suggested. "You never know how much help you're going to need out there."

Professor Robinson was already busy readying his equipment. "Mmm-hmm," he murmured.

Will took that as an okay. "I'll go down to the robot bay and help prepare him," Will offered.

Maureen smiled as she watched Will and the Robot leave the bridge. "Like father, like son," she said with a grin. "Be careful out there," she added.

"Aren't I always?" the professor replied.

"No," Maureen said softly. "So try this time, okay?"

He nodded and kissed her gently. Then Penny kissed her father and returned to the transmission console, choking back tears.

A few minutes later, Will took a seat beside Penny on the bridge. Maureen Robinson checked the controls. "Prepare to blast off," she broadcast into the probe's remote monitor. "Ten, nine, eight . . ." When Maureen reached one, Penny and Will felt a quick jerk of the *Jupiter 2* as the space probe blasted off. They watched through the giant window as their father floated off into space on yet another dangerous mission.

Will looked anxiously at his sister. "You know, Pen, there is a slight chance that Dr. Smith is right, that the creatures on board are dangerous aliens."

Penny shook her head. "Dr. Smith is never right!" she declared forcefully.

Will smiled weakly. There was a first time for everything. He just hoped this wasn't it.

5
The Rescue

"We have connected with the vessel," John Robinson's voice was clear and calm as it projected through the *Jupiter 2*'s broadcast speaker. "We're going inside."

Penny smiled. They'd arrived safely. The first stage of the mission was a success. Will was less enthusiastic than his sister. He knew the landing party still faced the most dangerous part of their mission — entering unknown territory.

Major West took the lead position, making sure he was the one to enter the rescue ship first. He opened the door and walked in slowly, his gun raised and ready. His blue eyes scanned the vehicle quickly for danger. He found none. In fact, he found nothing. There didn't appear to be anyone on board.

"You're not going to believe this," he told the others, who followed closely behind him.

"Try me," Dr. Smith replied in a droll voice.

"There's nobody here," Major West continued.

"But that's impossible," Judy said. "Someone had to be steering the ship toward the *Jupiter 2*."

Major West walked over to the rescue vessel's computer console. "It's on automatic pilot," he said, pointing to a direct

25

course button that had been set to coincide with the path of the *Jupiter 2*.

"The people on board the mother ship must have known they were about to self-destruct and launched this before their deaths," Professor Robinson deduced gravely.

The crew of the *Jupiter 2* stood silent, each member contemplating what it would be like to know one had only moments to survive.

"Isn't it odd that they didn't send anyone on the rescue ship?" Judy asked. "Why else would they have launched it?"

Dr. Smith rolled his eyes. "Why else, indeed. It's a trap, that's why. And we've fallen for it."

For once Dr. Smith had a thought the others could not necessarily write off to cowardice. The vessel had most definitely been launched for a purpose. The question was, was it launched as a rescue ship or as a war ship?

There was only one way to find out. The Robot, Professor Robinson, and Judy, followed by a reluctant Dr. Smith, carefully walked farther into the other ship. They moved gingerly around the vessel, searching for hidden booby traps. Luckily they didn't find any. But they didn't find any survivors, either.

"Well, what have we here?" Major West called out suddenly from the other side of the small bridge. "Judy, John, I think you'd better come here. Smith, stay where you are."

"Gladly," Dr. Smith replied.

Judy's eyes were questioning as she made her way over to Major West. He stood up and pointed slowly to a space just beneath the console. Judy bent down and peered into the darkness.

"Well, hello there," she said softly, climbing beneath the console. Professor Robinson followed closely behind. He held his gun at the ready.

"You can put the weapons away, Dad," Judy said. "I think we've discovered why the ship was launched. And I don't think these folks mean any harm."

Judy moved out of the way so her father could peer into the tiny space. There Professor Robinson came face-to-face with two children, a girl who appeared to be about eleven and a boy who looked about fifteen. The rescue vessel must have been launched to save the children of the doomed spaceship. John Robinson sighed. He knew that he would have done the exact same thing to save his own children's lives. And those could have been his kids — both children wore space uniforms with the United States flag sewn onto the upper right-hand pockets, just like Will's and Penny's.

Professor Robinson slowly held out his hands to the petrified children. "Hi. I'm John Robinson. It's okay now. We're here to help you."

The children huddled closer together, moving even further from the professor's reach.

"What are your names?" the professor asked them.

But the children were too afraid to speak. They blinked silently at John Robinson.

"Let me give it a try," Judy said to her dad. She gave the kids a deep smile. "You were very brave to go on board this ship by yourselves," she told them. "How about coming with us to our ship? We'll make sure you're safe. And we'll get you something to eat. Surely you've worked up an appetite after all this adventure."

But the children didn't respond to Judy, either. Robot wheeled himself behind her to analyze the situation. Judy was about to ask Major West to call the Robot back. She was afraid his flashing lights and dull whirring sound might upset the two children. But the strangest thing happened. When the little girl saw the Robot, her bright blue eyes lit up with excitement. She carefully took a few steps closer to the mechanical droid. Then she smiled weakly.

The older boy followed close behind the girl. He took her hand, and the two sidled up beside Robot. They rubbed his metal limbs carefully. Then they looked at Judy and nodded.

"That means you'll come with us, right?" Judy asked.

Again the children nodded.

"Well, if you're going to come on board, we at least have to know your names," Major West added. But the children did not reply.

Judy approached the little girl and checked her identification tag. It read Caitlin Johnson. The boy's tag read Carlos Gonzalez.

"Carlos, is there anyone else on board that we don't know about? Someone else who might need our help?" Judy asked.

The boy shook his head.

"It must have been very hard for you," Professor Robinson said. "But you're safe now. Come with us. We'll take care of you on board our ship, the *Jupiter 2*."

"Not so fast, Professor," Dr. Smith's stern voice rang through the small ship. "These children have not been thoroughly examined. They could be carrying a disease, or worse."

"All the more reason to bring them on board and care for them," Judy countered with authority. After all, she was a doctor, too.

"No, Judy, in this case I think Smith is correct. Much as I hate to admit it," Don West said. "We can't risk the lives of your family this way."

Judy sighed. West and Smith on the same side of an issue — Judy knew she was beaten. Reluctantly she pulled out a holographic scanner and waved it over the girl's body. Instantly the machine revealed images of her major organs and bones, and recorded her blood levels. Judy repeated the procedure with the boy. She studied the results for a minute. Then she ran the tests again.

Don West noted some concern in her face. "What's wrong, Judy?" he asked. "Something serious?"

Judy shook her head. "Nothing major, Major," she said with a laugh. "Their vital functions are all normal, although they seem to have been through an awful shock. It's their blood counts that are confusing me. The numbers are all normal except for their iron levels. Those are through the roof."

Dr. Smith stood tall. "See, I told you. There's something odd about all of this. It's probably some sort of space virus. Possibly contagious."

Judy shook her head in disagreement. She looked at her father. "I don't think it's any type of virus, Dad. High iron counts could be caused by a lot of things, none of them contagious or incurable."

Professor Robinson considered all of the information at hand. Then he nodded at Judy. "Bring them on board the *Jupiter 2*," he said. "They need us. We'll travel on board our probe and tow this one behind — just in case there's anything these two need, or any clues as to what happened to the others."

Judy smiled. "Come with me, you guys," she said. "I know some kids who are just dying to meet you."

"Interesting choice of words," Dr. Smith noted as they prepared to return to the *Jupiter 2*'s space probe.

6
The Passengers

The flashing light on the console indicated that the probe vehicle had docked once again. "Hey, they're back!" Will called out excitedly as he raced to meet the landing party.

"Whoa! Slow down, Will," John Robinson said as he and his son almost collided on the bridge. Then he turned to his wife. "We're back, safe and sound," he told her gently.

"And we've brought two visitors on board," Judy said. "I think Will and Penny will be especially interested in them."

Judy gently pushed the two children toward Will and Penny. "Penny, this is Carlos Gonzalez. Carlos, this is my sister, Penny."

Penny reached out her hand to shake Carlos's. He stared at it for a moment, then slapped it away. Penny was surprised, and angry. But one look at the fear in Carlos's deep brown eyes stopped her from saying anything. She just put her hand at her side and said, "Welcome aboard."

Carlos watched her intently. But he did not respond.

Will walked up to the girl, who looked about his age. "Hi! " he said excitedly.

"Hi!" the girl repeated in almost the exact same tone. Then

she jumped, as if she were surprised by the sound of her own voice.

"I'm Will Robinson," Will introduced himself. "Who are you?"

"I am uh . . . uh . . . uh," the girl stammered.

"Her name's Caitlin," Judy told Will, knowing that Caitlin was probably too traumatized to reply.

"You want to come and see the work I'm doing in the robot bay?" Will asked.

"Will, I don't think Caitlin is up to —" Judy began. But Caitlin interrupted her.

"Robots? Yes, Will, I would love to see them. I am a great fan of robotics," Caitlin said.

"Cool!" Will exclaimed. "I love robots, too. I guess you could say I'm a real metal head! Let's go down to the robot bay!"

Will looked over at his parents for permission to be excused. Professor Robinson nodded. There would be plenty of time to get the kids settled in later.

Will led Caitlin off the bridge and down to the robot bay on the lower level of the ship.

But things were not going quite as well with Penny and Carlos. Carlos stood silent and stoic, not knowing which way to turn.

"BLAWP! BLAWP! BLAWP!" Blawp began squealing loudly. She sniffed at Carlos's leg and jumped onto Penny's shoulder.

"Calm down, Blawp!" Penny demanded, cradling the small creature in her arms. Then she turned to apologize to Carlos. "She doesn't usually act this way," she explained. "I guess she's not used to strangers. We're the only humans she's ever known."

Carlos nodded slowly.

"Or maybe she knows something about these strangers that we don't," Dr. Smith muttered under his breath.

"So, uh, would you like to come look at our holographic image games?" Penny asked Carlos. "I've got some really good ones. And the equipment on board is the newest, so the smells match those on Earth pretty closely, and the physical interactions between us and the characters seem almost real. I thought these would be ten years old by the time I tried them again. But as it is, they're pretty current."

"Earth," Carlos repeated slowly.

"I know just how you feel. I've been kind of homesick for the old blue marble myself," Penny admitted. "Maybe interacting with people from home — even if they are just holograms — will make you feel better."

"Maybe," Carlos answered.

"I've also got some image cartridges from Earth's moon, if you're looking for some adventure."

"I think Earth would be fine," Carlos replied.

Penny led Carlos to the multiscreen hologram projection room.

Maureen and John grinned as they watched Penny leave with Carlos. "She sure looks happy," Maureen remarked. "Maybe we've heard the last of Penny Robinson, Space Captive. At least for awhile."

John laughed. "Will seemed glad to have a new friend, too. And she's interested in robots. A match made . . ."

". . . in the heavens," Maureen finished his thought as she stared off into space. "A lucky break for the kids, I'll say!"

"Not just for the kids," Professor Robinson suggested. "Lucky for us, too. Think about it. Maybe the ship blew up before we could ID it, but judging by the fact that those two kids speak American English and are wearing U.S. insignias, I'd venture a guess that their mother ship was one of ours. And judging from the age of that rescue vehicle they were in, their home ship was pretty old. It probably didn't have a hyperdrive function. So, they couldn't have gone too far from Earth's galaxy."

For a moment everyone on the deck was silent. It was too much to hope for.

"Pretty good news, huh, Judy?" Major West finally asked.

But Judy didn't reply. She was busy studying the results of Carlos's and Caitlin's blood tests. The numbers just weren't adding up. And those iron levels were dangerously high. She had to find out what the problem was and figure out how to fix it. If her calculations were correct, she didn't have much time. The iron counts were rapidly reaching toxic levels. The kids were heading for certain death.

Major West walked over and put his arm around Judy. "Still worried about those numbers?"

Judy nodded.

"Well, the best place to help those kids is at a hospital back home. So maybe we should all get to work trying to figure out whether or not we really are back in our own galaxy, and if we are, just how far from home we are."

Major West walked over to the navigation console. He studied it carefully. His face remained calm, but something in his eyes made Judy nervous. She watched as he fiddled with the buttons for a few minutes, then watched the screen again. Something was wrong.

"Okay, Major, spill it. What's going on?" she asked.

Don looked at the others. "Something's wrong with our navigational system. Some sort of magnetic force is throwing everything off. I can't get a definitive reading on our position."

He focused his attention on the system once again. It was

impossible to tell whether or not the ship was being pulled into the orbit of a planet or a large moon. And that was dangerous. Because now the only way to tell if the *Jupiter 2* was headed for a collision with another object was for the crew to spot it with their eyes. And by the time they spotted anything, it would probably be too late.

"Better put up the protective shields," Professor Robinson ordered.

"For how long, John?" Maureen asked. "Flying with protective shields can eat up a lot of power. Power we can't afford to lose."

John nodded slowly. "I know. But we have no choice. We'll have to disengage any nonessential systems until we can correct the navigational controls. Let's hope it won't take too long."

He stared out at the darkness that surrounded the ship. They'd have to be more alert than ever now. There was no telling what they were heading toward.

"Did anyone ever study the *Titanic* in history class?" Dr. Smith asked ominously. "I suggest you watch out for icebergs, Professor."

7
Friend or Foe?

For a few days, the adults managed to man the ship without the navigational equipment. And Penny, for one, was completely oblivious to any trouble. In fact, she was the happiest she'd been since the family had boarded the *Jupiter 2*. She and Carlos had become almost inseparable since the first day they'd met. They spent almost all of their free time together, listening to music and watching hours and hours of multiscreen sensory movies.

It was interesting for Penny to watch movies with Carlos. He always seemed to be seeing things for the first time. And watching Carlos made Penny feel as though she were seeing the films for the first time as well. Penny figured that they didn't have many sensory movies on his home ship, because every smell, sound, touch, and story seemed to fascinate him. She could see his big brown eyes open wide when a new scene passed on the screen, and his mind seemed to work like a computer, registering all the new sensations. It made Penny feel even closer to Carlos — like she was privileged to be such a big part of his new life.

Penny taught Carlos the latest dances (at least the dances

that were hot when the Robinsons had left Earth), and Carlos concentrated as hard on learning those as he did on the films. Penny was thrilled to have a dance partner on board.

The only problem in Penny and Carlos's friendship came whenever Penny would ask Carlos about his home life. He simply refused to discuss anything about his life before the destruction of his ship.

"It might help you feel better just to talk about it," Penny told Carlos during one of their marathon music listening sessions.

"It is simply not something I would like to discuss," Carlos replied. "Shall we listen to something else?"

Penny sighed. "I'm sure you miss your folks a lot," she noted.

"My folks?"

"Yeah, your folks. You know, your mom and dad?" Penny said.

"Oh, yes. My folks," Carlos repeated. "Penny, I would prefer not to speak about them. Is that all right with you?"

Penny agreed to drop the subject — for now. But later, she discussed the conversation with her older sister.

"It's the strangest thing, Judy. For a minute there I could swear Carlos had forgotten he had parents at all," Penny said as she helped Judy inventory the medicines in the sick bay.

"It's quite possible he has," Judy replied. "Severe trauma like this can cause a kind of amnesia. But even if he has forgotten everyone he has ever known, it may come back to him."

"How can I help that happen?" Penny asked.

"Keep doing what you're doing. Be a friend who's willing to listen," Judy told her.

Penny nodded. That wouldn't be too hard. She really liked Carlos. It was great having someone her own age around.

*   *   *

Will, on the other hand, was miserable. He, too, was unaware of any mechanical malfunctions on board the *Jupiter 2*, but that was because he'd been spending most of his time trying to ditch Caitlin.

At first Will had liked Caitlin. She seemed interested in hearing his theories on robotics, and she really enjoyed playing holographic chess. It was fun for Will to play chess with someone who, unlike Robot, had human foibles. But Caitlin had a mind like a steel trap, and she had already memorized some of Will's most classic moves. Worse yet, Caitlin was a very lousy winner, worse than Robot. And her gloating really got to Will.

After a few days of Caitlin's constant companionship, Will had had enough of their togetherness. Caitlin was getting on his nerves!

She insisted on following Will all over the ship, asking him detailed questions about his robots and making him show her all of his equipment. She was like Will's shadow, following him everywhere but the bathroom. (And Will was pretty sure she would have gone there, too, if he hadn't locked the door.) No matter where they went, Will got the creepy feeling that somehow Caitlin was taking mental notes — as if she was trying to act like Will or something, like she had to learn how to be human all over again. Will usually tried to bring Caitlin down to the robot bay as often as possible. If she was going to try and copy him, at least she could help him do some of his repair work on the ship's small robot crew.

"What is this?" Caitlin asked, lifting a small metal oval out of Will's tool capsule.

"That's a spare microchip odometer. It measures the exact number of meters a robot has traveled. I have to give them all a complete system run-through every two thousand kilometers or so. Sometimes even more often if the terrain on a given planet is especially rugged. Hey, can you hand me that Allen wrench over there?"

Caitlin searched the capsule. "I do not see an Allen wrench," she replied.

Will sighed. Caitlin wasn't very much help. She probably didn't even know what an Allen wrench was.

"It's right there, next to the microchip drill bits. . . ." Will began. Then he looked into the tool capsule. Caitlin was right. The iron-coated L-shaped wrench wasn't there. But it had been there a minute ago, Will was sure of it.

"Where'd you put the wrench?" Will asked accusingly.

"I do not know what you are speaking about," Caitlin replied. "Here, try using this electrode grip instead."

Will grabbed the smaller tool from Caitlin's hand and began turning a screw inside a small remote robot.

"Perhaps it would be easier if you did it this way," Caitlin said slowly. She reached in with her bare hands and twisted the screw to the right. It came undone in an instant.

Will stared at her in amazement. "How did you do that?" Will asked.

Caitlin turned away nervously. "I am sorry. Did I do something wrong?"

"No, not wrong, just incredible," Will said. "What are you, superhuman?"

"Superhuman? No, not at all," Caitlin replied. "I am just very strong."

Will scowled. The girl was such a show-off. He went back and removed the front plate from the small droid. Then he began testing each of its wires for damage.

Caitlin watched over his shoulder for awhile. Then she

38

walked over to examine a shelf full of minidroids, programmed to perform various small tasks around the spaceship. "What are these made of?" she asked as she gently caressed the arm of one of the shinier droids.

"Those are all steel," Will said. "They have to be. It's the only way they can endure the pressure and weight of some of the things they have to lift."

Caitlin nodded slowly. "And that one?" She pointed toward Will's Robot.

"Robot's exterior is aluminum casing," he said slowly. "But inside he's pure iron. Only the best for him."

"Iron. Hmmm. That reminds me. I am extremely hungry."

Will stared at Caitlin. Where did that come from? "Uh, you want some chocolate ice cream?" Will asked. "I could open a cold pack or something."

Caitlin shook her head. "Ice cream? No, that is okay. I will take something in my room."

"Suit yourself," Will said. He wiped the sweat from his forehead and looked at his grease-covered hands. "I'd better go, too. I have to shower before dinner." He headed slowly toward the exit of the robot bay. "You coming?" he asked Caitlin as he left.

"I will be upstairs in a moment," Caitlin called after him.

Something in Caitlin's expression made Will nervous. "I, uh, don't usually like people down here without me. It's, uh, kind of my responsibility and if anything happened . . ." Will stammered before letting his words trail off.

"Oh. All right, Will. I'm coming." And with that Caitlin moved through the door behind Will and Robot. As Will turned to press his entry/exit code into the door lock, he had the strangest feeling that Caitlin was staring over his shoulder.

8
The Cover-up

It wasn't until late that night that Will and Robot finally got some time alone. Will looked forward to his private time with Robot. It was nice to have someone to talk to — someone who didn't bug him or treat him like a little kid.

"There's something strange about that girl, Robot," Will told his buddy.

"I do detect some disparity in her chemical makeup," Robot agreed.

"No, that's just her iron levels. Judy's working on that. There's something else wrong. I mean, listen to how she talks. She doesn't sound like a kid. And how about the way she loosened that screw with her bare hands? I can't explain it with facts. It's just a feeling I have."

"I am not programmed to feel," Robot said plainly.

"I know. I'm working on a human emotion replication program for you," Will assured him.

"But my main computer is programmed to replicate the human thinking process," Robot continued. "And you know what I am programmed to think about girls. . . ."

"I know," Will said with a smile.

40

"Girls are danger, Will Robinson," Robot continued.

Will laughed. He had programmed Robot to say that. He continued to think about the two new visitors on board. The more he thought about it, the stranger they seemed.

The next afternoon, Will and Caitlin joined Penny and Carlos to watch a multichoice make-your-own movie. Will chose the beginning. He picked a comedy-adventure like those old-time comedies his great-great-grandmother had loved. The movie started out with slapstick moments: actors whacking into doors and slipping on banana peels. After awhile, Penny switched the program to a musical comedy. Usually Will hated musical comedies. But today he didn't care. He wasn't watching the movie, anyway. He was too busy watching Caitlin and Carlos watch the movie. Their reactions to the film were very strange. It was almost as though they had no sense of humor. Not a bad sense of humor, but no sense of humor at all! Caitlin and Carlos would watch the movie, observe a funny scene, and then watch for Penny's reaction. If she giggled, they giggled. If she chuckled, they chuckled. And if she guffawed, they did the same — in a stilted, studied manner.

A man on the screen reached over and put his arm around his date. Will could see Carlos studying this carefully. Then, slowly and mechanically, the older boy lifted his arm and dropped it heavily over Penny's shoulders. Penny smiled contentedly. Will frowned. Carlos couldn't even come up with *that* one on his own! Why couldn't Penny see that Carlos was just imitating the guy on the screen?

Yes, something was really off with these two. Will decided to test their reactions. He quietly sidled his way toward the remote control. He pushed two buttons and stared at the screen. Suddenly the movie took a different turn. It seamlessly went from comedy to drama. Will had changed the movie in midstream. But because the actors were the same, no one seemed to notice.

Suddenly, the heroine of the movie turned to face an evil attacker. There was a shot of light from the attacker's laser gun. The heroine gasped and fell to the ground, dead.

At first, Carlos and Caitlin laughed, just as they had when the detective had landed headfirst in a chocolate cream pie. But when they noticed that Will and Penny had not laughed at all, they studied Penny's expression and mimicked her shock, then sadness. Tears even appeared in their eyes.

Will confronted Penny with this latest bit of data as the two headed off to join the rest of the crew for dinner.

"It was weird, Pen, I swear," Will insisted to his sister. "It was as if they had no real emotions. Like they were trained androids or something."

Penny shook her head adamantly. "You're imagining things, little bro. We already know they're not aliens. Judy could have figured that out from their first medical exams. Maybe they're just so shaken up from everything they've been through that they have no real emotions left. Shock can do that to a person, you know."

But Will didn't buy it. "Okay, so why don't they ever eat with us? They always grab something to munch on in their cabins while the rest of us eat together."

Penny stopped walking and stared at her brother intently. "How can you be so uncaring, Will Robinson?! Here we are eating happily with our entire family, while they have no family left at all. How do you think you would feel if you were suddenly an orphan?"

Will scuffed his shoe against the floor. All right, he felt properly chastised. For a minute, anyway. Then he remembered something else that was bothering him about the new visitors.

"Okay, Penny, so explain to me why they never take showers," Will countered. "Some sort of odd memory about rain showers back on Earth?"

Penny shrugged. "I give up on you, Will. Of course they take showers. They've been on board for almost a week already. If they hadn't showered, they'd be pretty disgusting by now. And I don't think Carlos or Caitlin are disgusting. What's your theory, science brain — that they melt when they're hit by water? Maybe they're related to the Wicked Witch of the West. You know, that character from those Oz books we read in classic lit class."

"I'm telling you, Penny, they don't shower."

Penny shook her head. "No, Will, that's *your* fantasy. You may not like showering, but other people do. They probably just do it late at night when the rest of us are asleep, to assure themselves plenty of privacy."

Will sighed. This wasn't working. Then he looked down and noticed Blawp sitting at Penny's feet. Blawp squawked and ran out of the room every time she came into contact with Caitlin or Carlos.

"What about Blawp, Pen? Why does she go crazy every time she sees Carlos and Caitlin?"

Penny took a deep breath. "I don't know, Will. Maybe she's jealous of the time I spend with Carlos. Or . . ."

"Or what, Penny?" he asked.

"Or nothing, Will. Are you going to base your whole theory on the reactions of an alien creature? Not very scientific." Penny hooked her small, shell-shaped music implant into her left ear, adjusted the volume, and walked away in exasperation.

Will frowned. He wasn't getting anywhere with Penny. She obviously had a crush on Carlos. The other night Will had caught her sending a holographic image of herself to his room. It must have contained a recorded love message or something. Penny wanted a friend so badly that she couldn't see that this guy was incredibly boring. A real dud. He seemed like he was nothing but an empty shell with a voice.

Still, Will was determined to get through to his sister. Otherwise, she might get herself into trouble.

She might get them all into trouble.

As Will and Penny turned the corner to the dining quarters, Will overheard the grown-ups talking.

"Any change in status, Major?" Professor Robinson asked.

"I'm afraid not, John," Major West replied. "The navigational systems still aren't working. I keep getting wacky readings with no indication of where we are or what we're near."

"Well, then, for the time being, we will remain on manual alert," Professor Robinson declared. "Who's on emergency lookout now?"

"Judy," Maureen replied. "I'll take over for her on the bridge after dinner."

The adults became silent as Will and Penny entered the room. Will looked at them curiously. "What's going on?" he asked suspiciously.

Maureen smiled brightly. "Nothing much," she said. "What's going on with you?"

"Where's Judy?" Will asked.

"She's, um, in sickbay, looking at Carlos's and Caitlin's latest blood test results," Maureen answered after a moment's hesitation. "She'll grab a bite later. Here are your food packs, kids. Dig in."

She placed a ration pack on Will's plate. Then she passed one to Penny.

"Penny, how many times do I have to ask you not to

wear your music implant at the table?" Maureen warned her daughter.

Penny looked at her mother with amazement. The implant was so tiny, it was impossible to detect under her hair. Sometimes she thought her mother had developed a secret sixth sense while visiting one of the alien planets they'd landed on.

Penny removed the shell-like device from her ear. Then she looked down at her food pack and scowled. Ugh. It was banana beef again.

Will slowly opened his ration pack and looked at his mother. Something weird was going on. His mother seemed overly cheerful, and the smiles on Major West's and his father's faces were tight and unbending, as if they were glued in place or something. Only Dr. Smith resembled his usual grumpy self. To top it all off, Will had specifically overheard his mother say that she would replace Judy on lookout on the bridge. Not in the sickbay. So what was his mother covering up?

Something very strange was going on aboard the *Jupiter 2*, and Will was going to get to the bottom of it if it killed him.

He just hoped that it wouldn't.

9
Spy Mission

That night, after dinner, Will deliberately avoided Caitlin. He raced down to the robot bay and locked the door. Then he spoke quietly to Robot.

"Look, buddy, something strange is going on on this ship, and I want to know what it is. But if I go around spying, the grown-ups are going to start acting weird again. I'm pretty sure there's something they don't want Penny and me to know about. But they'll talk freely in front of you, so you're going to have to do the spying for me."

Will reached into a backpack he was carrying and removed a small holographic lens. He expertly opened Robot's front panel. He inserted the lens onto the holographic camera that was already part of Robot's makeup. This new lens would guarantee a stronger holographic image and clearer voice reception. Will did not want to miss a thing. Next, Will rearranged the Robot's frontal plate to allow the camera complete mobility. Finally, he closed up the panel.

"I want you to stay up on the bridge and project images back here to me," Will told Robot. "And make sure you stay within sound recording range of Dad and Major West at all times."

"Roger, Will Robinson. I will gather information from the instruments and crew of the *Jupiter 2*," Robot confirmed.

"You got it!" Will declared. "Now go to the bridge."

Will watched as the bubble-headed Robot wheeled away to the turbo lift that would take him to the grown-ups. As Will sat, waiting for images of his parents, Judy, and Major West to be transmitted to the robot bay, he felt kind of guilty. He really didn't like spying — at least not on his mom and dad.

From the moment Robot entered the bridge area, Will knew he was correct about the grown-ups' reaction. They never even looked up to greet him. The adults always seemed to relate to Robot as though he were just another piece of mechanical equipment. But Will knew he was more.

As Robot carefully eyed the ship's controls, holographic images of his father and Major West appeared in the robot bay. Will could see and hear his father's and Major West's images conferring anxiously.

"There's a magnetic force out there that's throwing the controls off," Will heard Major West say. "At least I think it's out there. Sometimes the numbers make it seem as though the magnets are being pulled by some sort of force inside the ship."

"That's highly unlikely. It's got to be coming from outside. The question is, from where?" Professor Robinson responded.

Will jumped. So that was it. Their navigational controls weren't working properly.

"Well, luckily we haven't spotted any planets or objects that could pull us into an unsafe orbit," Maureen's holographic image added. "Do you think the ship is staying on course?"

"It's impossible to tell," Major West replied.

Will had heard all he needed to hear. He used his remote control to call Robot back to the robot bay. The Robot turned and immediately left the bridge. The adults never even knew he was there.

When Robot returned, Will prepared for part two of his spy mission.

"I'm not sure how or why . . . yet," Will told Robot. "But I think Major West was right. I'll bet the problem with the navigational controls is on board the ship. I think the problem is somehow tied in to Caitlin and Carlos being on board. But that's just a feeling, and Mom and Dad will want scientific evidence. So I need you to follow Caitlin and Carlos around for awhile, and find out everything you can about them."

Robot's lights blinked on and off as he absorbed Will's commands. Will waited a second and then continued.

"This time I want you to go and spy on those two and send their images into my room. I'll record them and we can analyze the data together, later."

"Roger, Will Robinson," Robot agreed. "I will find the passengers and send their holographic images to your room."

Will followed Robot out of the robot bay. As Robot headed to the cargo bay area — which was being used as a cabin for Carlos and Caitlin — Will went to his room to wait for the holographic images to appear.

Robot was gone a long time. Fifteen minutes. Twenty minutes. Half an hour. But still no images of Carlos and Caitlin appeared in Will's room.

Finally Robot returned to Will's room. He rolled in slowly and stood at attention in front of Will.

"So what happened to the images? Did you find those two?" Will asked.

"Which two?" Robot answered mysteriously.

"Carlos and Caitlin, of course," Will said. Was this some sort of joke?

"Carlos," Robot began. "A name of Spanish origin, meaning one who is strong and manly. Caitlin. A name of —"

"I don't care what their names mean!" Will interrupted angrily. "What I want to know is, did you notice either of them exhibiting any behavior that was not quite . . . human?"

The Robot turned quickly toward Will's door. He must have turned too quickly, because part of his left arm broke off and landed with a bang on the floor.

Will reached over and picked up the body part. He took out his tool kit and prepared to reinstall it. But as Will removed his screwdriver, he noticed something strange. The iron screw that held the arm to the Robot's body had been broken in two, and only the lower part of the screw remained. There were a few other small pieces of metal missing from the arm as well. The holographic lens was broken and separated from the camera. That explained why no images had been broadcast to his room.

"How'd that happen?" Will murmured as he replaced the broken screw and removed the lens.

Will could see that he was not going to get any new information from Robot today. For a split second he thought about telling Robot exactly what to look for and sending him back to Caitlin's and Carlos's cabins, but he figured that they might get suspicious if Robot visited them twice in one evening. And besides, Will wasn't quite sure what he wanted to know. No, Will would have to wait another day before he could send Robot out on another spy mission. But that left a whole evening with nothing to do. So Will decided to challenge Robot to yet another game of holographic chess.

Will set up the chess set and made the first move using his bishop's pawn. The game progressed normally at first. And then Will made a mistake. He left his queen open to capture by Robot's knight. Will bit his lip, frustrated at the stupidity of the move. He figured it was just about over. Once Robot captured his queen, Will would be in check, with very few moves left until checkmate.

But then the strangest thing happened. Robot didn't move his knight. He moved a pawn instead, leaving Will's queen safely in place.

At first, Will was thrilled. But then he was worried. Robot didn't make mistakes like that. The only way Robot could lose a chess game was if Will played better than he did. And Will knew he wasn't playing well.

Will's mind started racing. Everything was just too weird. First, Robot hadn't followed his instructions but instead had reported on the origin of Carlos's name. Then he lost at a chess game — a chess game that he definitely should have won.

Maybe Will had knocked something loose when he installed the holographic lens. But that was impossible, because Robot had seemed fine while Will was explaining what he needed him to do when he spied on Caitlin and Carlos. But now Robot seemed totally confused. Something had happened to him. The question was, what?

Will thought back. Maybe Penny had reprogrammed the Robot. Could she be trying to get back at him for those cracks he'd made about Robot being the closest thing she'd find to a boyfriend? But that didn't make sense. Penny had a boyfriend now — that weirdo, Carlos. Besides, Penny liked Robot. She felt, as Will did, that there was something almost human about him. And Penny didn't have it in her to hurt anything that was alive.

But who else? Well, there was Dr. Smith. Dr. Smith knew plenty about robots. He was the one who'd programmed Robot to kill the Robinsons when the *Jupiter 2* had first been launched into space. Dr. Smith was always threatening to tear Robot apart and use him for scrap metal. He was forever insisting that he needed a gun to protect himself. He could make a gun out of robot parts quite easily.

But as a prisoner, Dr. Smith was not entitled to any gun at all. And somehow, Will knew that even Dr. Smith wouldn't be willing to risk Major West's wrath by constructing his own gun. Major West was looking for any excuse to knock off Dr. Smith. Self-defense against a prisoner with a gun would be a pretty good one.

It had to be Carlos and Caitlin. Caitlin had taken a big interest in Robot. She had spent a lot of time in the robot bay, watching Will work on Robot's circuits. And Robot had been on a mission in Carlos's and Caitlin's quarters when this all started.

Brriinnnng!! Brrriiing! Brrriiing! Will didn't have any time to analyze the situation further. The alarm bell began ringing wildly throughout the halls of the *Jupiter 2*. Something was wrong. Will began to make his way to the bridge to find out what was going on, but the sound of his father's voice booming through the halls of the *Jupiter 2* stopped him right in his tracks.

"Assume emergency crash positions!" Professor Robinson's order blared over the ship's speakers. "I repeat, assume emergency crash positions. This is not a drill!"

10
Emergency!

Will raced back to his room and buckled himself into an emergency chair. He could feel the ship moving at a faster pace now, rocking wildly through space. At times like these, Robot wasn't the best companion. After all, he couldn't feel fear, so he couldn't give comfort or moral support. He tried, of course, but there was something about comfort from a Robot that just wasn't that comforting. Right now Will felt far away from the rest of his family.

SLAM! The *Jupiter 2* smashed into something with enormous force. Will lunged forward, but the shoulder harness kept him from falling to the ground. Will rubbed at his shoulder. He was going to have one nasty bruise tomorrow — if there was a tomorrow. Suddenly everything went dark, and the temperature in the room dropped dramatically.

"Emergency life-support systems now activated." Will could hear his mother's calm voice ringing out over the intercom system. Just hearing it made Will feel a lot better.

The ship bumped around a few more times and then came to an abrupt halt. The lights flickered on and off and then finally

stayed on. Will sat motionless, afraid to unhook his harness —
and afraid not to. He wanted to be with the rest of his family.

"Will, are you okay?" Penny shouted from her cabin next to
his.

Will smiled. Now he knew his mother and Penny were okay.
"Yeah, I'm fine, Pen," Will answered. He looked over at Robot.
The metal droid had fallen hard against the floor. His bubble-
shaped head was tilted and his circuits seemed to be damaged.
"Robot's a little banged up, though," Will added.

"You can fix him later," Penny reassured him.

"How's Blawp?" Will asked his sister.

"Blawp! Blawp!" Blawp let out a squeal at the sound of her
name. Will and Penny both laughed.

"I guess that means she's okay," Penny told Will. Then she
called out to Carlos and Caitlin. There was no answer.

"Carlos!" Penny repeated anxiously. "Caitlin?"

Nothing but silence. Then Will heard footsteps coming down
the hall. The footsteps were followed by the loud, wild blawping of Blawp. Will laughed in spite of himself. Blawp was be-
coming a scaly-skinned guard dog, blawping out warnings of
approaching weirdos.

Will looked past his door and saw Carlos and Caitlin
strolling calmly by. They don't even know they are supposed
to be frightened, Will thought.

But they figured it out pretty quickly. "What are you two
doing walking around?" Penny demanded, her voice shaking
with anxiety. "Get back in the bay! Dad hasn't told us to release our harnesses yet."

Almost instantly, the two of them began to tremble, just as
Will was trembling. Then, before Penny could say more, the
two newcomers raced back to their quarters.

Weird, Will thought. This is dangerously weird.

After a few minutes, Will's mom came tearing into his cabin. "Are you okay?" she asked him.

"My shoulder's a little bruised from the harness," Will said. "Nothing major."

"Go down to sickbay and have Judy or Dr. Smith take a look at it, honey," Maureen said. "I'll go check on the other kids."

"Wait!.You can't go yet, Mom. You've got to tell me what happened."

Maureen nodded. "Okay, here it is. We've been having a little trouble with the navigational system. We just collided with a rather large moon, and we're currently stuck on the moon's surface."

"How much damage to the *Jupiter 2* is there?" Will asked.

"I'm not sure, honey. Dad and Major West are checking on that right now. Now get yourself down to sickbay. And while you're at it, take Robot down to the robot bay. Looks like he could use a tune-up."

Will did as he was told. He headed to sickbay immediately.

Judy wasn't there, but Dr. Smith was.

"Nice bruise, Will," Dr. Smith murmured. "I can't believe your parents have gotten us all into this mess. I warned them that bringing those alien children on board would cause trouble. But did they believe me? No! No one ever believes me."

Will looked at Dr. Smith with surprise. In some ways it felt nice to know that he wasn't the only one who thought there was something weird about Caitlin and Carlos. On the other hand, it felt kind of strange to actually agree with Dr. Smith.

"What makes you think they're aliens?" Will asked in a sly tone.

"They just don't seem as bratty as real human children," Dr. Smith replied in an equally cagey manner. He applied a warming salve on Will's injured shoulder. "Now run along and stay out of trouble."

After leaving sickbay, Will followed his mother's second order. He carefully led Robot to the robot bay and began to assess and repair his damages. Will laid the metal android down and carefully realigned his clear bubble-head. Instantly lights flashed on and off inside the Robot's dome.

"Twinkle, twinkle, little star. Its fleece was white as snow," Robot recited.

Will stared at his metal friend. Robot had obviously taken a harder hit than Will had originally thought. Something was really wrong now. Robot's intellectual network was programmed to analyze advanced space systems in a matter of seconds — and now he couldn't even get a simple nursery rhyme right.

Quickly Will opened the Robot's front plate. He searched the circuit board for a crossed wire or an overloaded circuit. Either one of those could have caused Robot's problems.

Once Will removed the plate entirely, he gasped. Someone — or something — had literally eaten through the internal wiring. And whatever it was hadn't stopped there. It had taken a few bites from the screws holding the circuit breakers together, too.

If Will hadn't known better, he'd swear that some sort of superstrong alien mouse had been nibbling on Robot's wires. It was the only explanation he could think of.

Logically, of course, Will knew there were no rodents on board the *Jupiter 2*. Still, Will smelled a rat — or two.

And he figured those rats were named Caitlin and Carlos.

11
A Secret Disclosed

Soon after the crash, Professor Robinson called a meeting of the crew and passengers of the *Jupiter 2*. Will knew he was supposed to come immediately when his father paged him for a meeting, but he didn't want to leave Robot in such a state of disarray. He fiddled with the wires a few minutes more, until he was satisfied with the Robot's condition.

When he arrived on the bridge, everyone else was already there. And the look on his father's face let Will know that he wasn't pleased with his tardiness.

"Sorry I'm late, Dad," Will apologized breathlessly as he took his place at the table. "I was busy fixing up Robot's circuits. Something had eaten through all of his wiring." Will glared at Caitlin and Carlos, but they didn't seem to have heard him.

Professor Robinson looked strangely at his son. He must have wondered what Will was talking about but he didn't say anything. Will knew his dad had a lot on his mind just then so he didn't say anything else about the Robot.

"We are now resting on the dark side of a small moon," Professor Robinson began. "We have not yet been able to identify the planet around which this moon rotates, but we are fairly certain of the moon's stability. Major West and I have run a full check of the *Jupiter 2*'s systems, and it appears that the damage to the ship is minimal. We can have the external damage fixed in a few hours.

"Unfortunately, the navigational instruments that would have helped us avoid this collision have failed. And we cannot seem to right them. Some sort of magnetic pull is causing the navigational compasses to malfunction."

Carlos raised his hand. "Maybe the moon's surface is metallic in makeup. That would throw your equipment off," he suggested eagerly.

A little too eagerly, Will thought.

"We thought of that, too," Maureen Robinson told Carlos. "But my initial tests would refute that hypothesis. The moon's makeup appears to be rock — granite mostly."

Carlos's face fell.

"Hey, don't be so bummed," Penny told him. "You can't be right all the time. That was an excellent educated guess. Mom's always telling us that educated guesses are the backbones of science."

But Carlos did not seem cheered.

"Anyway," Professor Robinson continued, "we're stuck here for the time being. We will not leave this moon until we can determine the cause of the problem with the navigational equipment and come up with a solution."

Penny groaned. Will knew she was thinking they'd never get back to Earth at this rate.

"Since the ship will not be in motion, certain systems will be on emergency power," Professor Robinson went on. "For instance, we will limit all water. Showers will be rationed to one every three days. . . ."

"No problem for you, huh, Caitlin?" Will whispered loudly into the girl's ear. Penny kicked him under the table.

"Luckily, the temperature will remain relatively constant, so we shouldn't perspire too badly," Maureen Robinson added, giving Will a stern warning look. "All music should be played on your ear modules only. They require far less power than the external broadcast equipment you guys have. And you should cool it on the holographic imagery games for awhile."

Now all four children groaned. What could be more boring than floating around in space without any holographic locations to visit?

"On the other hand, we can't use the computers for anything other than maintaining the ship. So we won't have that visual biology quiz we were scheduled for," Maureen went on.

This time Will and Penny cheered.

"Okay, you kids are all dismissed," Professor Robinson said.

Will waited until Penny, Carlos, and Caitlin had left the bridge. Then he moved alongside his father and dropped his voice to a whisper.

"Dad, I think there's something really weird about Carlos and Caitlin. And I think if we can figure out what they're up to, we'll be able to fix the navigational controls."

Professor Robinson shook his head with annoyance. "Look, Will," he said, "I don't know what kind of argument you've had with Caitlin and Carlos. But I advise you to patch it up immediately. I don't have time for this kind of nonsense right now."

Will jumped back. Nonsense? Lately his father had been receptive to all of his ideas. But that was before Caitlin and Carlos had boarded the *Jupiter 2*.

Deep in his heart, Will knew he was right about the two new

passengers. And he would prove it. The question was how to prove it. He left the bridge with a heavy sigh.

Will sat in his room and tried to come up with a list of the clues he already had. He knew that Caitlin was crazy about robots. He also knew that whatever had happened to Robot happened in the cargo bay Caitlin and Carlos shared.

From the corner of his eye, Will spotted Robot. He hated to sacrifice his friend's safety, but Will knew there was no other way to trap Carlos and Caitlin. He would have to send Robot back to their cargo bay quarters.

Before long, Will had prepared Robot for his mission. Because he had not had time to repair the holographic camera in Robot's front panel, he knew he would have to depend on his pal's photographic memory.

"There's no pressure this time, buddy," Will told the Robot. "Just memorize everything you see in the room. Then return and tell me what they said, what they're wearing, what they're reading, everything."

"Roger, Will Robinson," Robot replied. "I will return with the requested information." Then Robot rolled off on his assigned mission. As soon as the Robot was out of sight, Will started on part two of his plan.

First, Will put on a pair of cushiony sneakers. Then he quietly snuck down the hall to the cargo bay. The door was shut tight, but Will could hear a song by the Asteroids, a loud computer-generated music group, blaring from inside. The sound of the music infuriated Will. Hadn't Caitlin and Carlos heard his mother ask everyone to cool it on the unnecessary equipment? It was just like those two to put them all in danger of a serious power drain. They were seriously warped.

Will put his ear to the cabin door. He could hear Caitlin and

59

Carlos laughing. But their laughter wasn't the loose, relaxed giggling of two ordinary kids, or the imitation laughter they had tried to copy from Will and Penny earlier that week. Now it sounded like a rough, gravelly rumbling. It was inhuman, and it made Will nervous. Then Will realized that he didn't hear Robot at all. And that made him even more nervous.

He bent down and tried to peek through the keyhole in the cabin door. He couldn't see a thing. Will was frustrated. That trick always seemed to work in spy novels. There was nothing else to do but open the cabin door. Ever so slowly, Will eased the doorknob around and gave a slight push. The door opened a crack and he peered inside.

Luckily, both Caitlin and Carlos had their backs to the door. The loud music masked any sound Will might have made as he padded quietly into the room. Will took a quick look around. The room seemed extremely neat. There were no clothes strewn around on the floor and the bed was perfectly made. This definitely did not look like a normal kid's room. (No matter what Penny might say.)

Even from behind, Will could tell that Carlos and Caitlin were eating. And for just that one moment, Will began to doubt his own beliefs. Maybe they really were just unhappy kids. Hadn't Penny told him that Carlos and Caitlin were eating in their own quarters to avoid watching the Robinsons enjoy meals together?

Will was about to leave the room. Maybe he could get out of there without being discovered. He was already at the door when he heard a loud crunching noise. And it definitely wasn't the sound of space popcorn. It sounded more like the crunching of metal. Will took one last glance over at Carlos and Caitlin. And that's when he saw Robot.

The metal droid was lying in a crumpled heap in the middle of the floor. His head was still attached to his upper body, but his limbs had been separated. Large, sawlike teethmarks covered his left leg and his right arm. The shock of it all made Will forget he was spying.

"ROBOT! What have these monsters done to you?" Will screamed.

The sound of Will's voice belting out over the loud music startled Caitlin and Carlos. They dropped their food and turned suddenly. Will froze at the sight of them. From the back, Carlos and Caitlin had looked as they always did. But when they turned around, their true evil selves were revealed to Will for the first time. It was a sight no human being could ever be prepared for.

Caitlin's blue eyes had been replaced with red-hot flames. Her once pale skin was now a ruddy red, with dark brown rustlike patches scattered all over her body. As she opened her mouth to speak, rows of sharp, sharklike teeth emerged. Her long, thin, fork-shaped tongue hissed wildly in anger.

Carlos stood and stretched his body to all of its sinewy six feet. His eyes glowed like burning embers. He opened his mouth and licked his sharp razorlike fangs with his pointed tongue. Then he let loose with a loud, deep growl that made Will's skin crawl.

"What are you doing in this cabin?" the Caitlin-monster demanded. Her voice was no longer high-pitched and childlike. Instead it was deep, metallic, and foreboding.

The robotic sound of Caitlin's voice shocked Will back into action. He was afraid. He wanted to run. But he knew he could not leave his best friend here to die. Will tried to keep his arm from shaking as he pointed to the pile of nuts and bolts in the middle of the floor. "What have you two done to my Robot?" he demanded.

"We needed a food source. Your Robot provided the nutrients we were seeking," Caitlin hissed.

Will stared at her incredulously. "Y-Y-You mean you've been eating Robot? What are you guys, some sort of animals?"

Carlos's eyes flashed angrily. "We were merely doing what we needed to stay alive. Food packs filled with freeze-dried beef and fruits aren't going to sustain us. Believe us, your Robot was not our first choice. We tried to survive on any tiny nuts or bolts we could find around the ship, but our iron levels were getting dangerously low."

Will shook his head. He wasn't really interested in the passengers' iron levels right now. He looked over at his injured Robot, with his arms and legs strewn all over the floor. The flashing lights in his chest cavity were growing dim, and the dull whirring sound that indicated that his systems were working was almost completely silent. Will's eyes filled with tears.

Logically, Will should have run for help right then. But logic has very little to do with friendship. And Robot was the best friend Will had ever had. Quickly he went over and began gathering Robot's dismembered body parts.

"It will be okay, pal, I promise," Will said as he picked up Robot's left leg. "I'll fix you up as soon as we can get to the robot bay."

Behind him, Will could hear Carlos turn up the music even louder. Will's heart thumped wildly as he picked up the pieces of Robot. He knew Carlos was turning up the sound so that no one would hear if he screamed. But Will didn't scream. For one thing, he wasn't totally certain that Caitlin and Carlos were going to harm him. They must know that injuring him was a

62

surefire way for them to be discovered. Sooner or later his parents would come looking for him — even if they hadn't heard him scream.

Will took a calculated risk and stayed put. And then he heard the words he had been dreading.

"Danger, Will Robinson!" Robot warned in a voice that was barely a whisper. "Danger!"

12
The Perfect Host

Will looked over his shoulder. Caitlin hovered menacingly above him, holding Robot's right leg high over her head. She was prepared to slam the thick metal robotic limb right into Will's skull.

"No!" Will cried out. He jumped to his feet and ran toward the door. He had to get help. Fast!

But Carlos was quicker on his feet than Will was. He easily beat Will to the door. Carlos spread his arms across the open doorway and blocked the exit.

"We are sorry, Will. But now that you know our secret, we cannot let you go. We will have to kill you to ensure your silence," Carlos said matter-of-factly as he closed the door. Will struggled to keep his cool. If Major West had taught Will one thing, it was to make sure the enemy never saw you sweat. Major West said that enemies can smell fear, just like dogs. And they were certain to use it to their advantage. Keeping calm under stress confused their signals.

"You can't kill me," Will said in the calmest voice he could muster. "My parents would come looking for me, and eventually they'd find me here. You'd be in big trouble then."

"No problem." Caitlin laughed haughtily. "For one thing, your parents would never suspect anything bad from two sweet orphan children. Besides, we will simply blame the whole thing on your Robot. We will tell everyone that he had obviously gone berserk, and when you tried to disable him, a battle ensued."

"My folks would never fall for that," Will insisted. "They know Robot isn't programmed to kill."

"Well, anything can happen during a crash," Carlos reasoned. "But it is no matter. We have always assumed that we might have to kill the rest of them sooner or later, anyway."

Will gasped. Kill all of them? Why?

Caitlin waved Robot's leg in the air. "I will make this as painless as possible, because you've been such a nice host — or at least, you are about to be a nice host. . . ."

Will didn't have time to wonder what Caitlin was talking about. He was too busy racing around the cabin, trying to avoid her wildly swinging arms. Will ran away from the door and toward the far wall. Caitlin followed close behind. Will slammed his body into a small red button on the wall. Then he ricocheted onto the opposite wall. A series of deafening alarms sounded in the hallway. Will had engaged the emergency call button that was on the wall of every cabin in the *Jupiter 2*.

Judy was the first to arrive on the scene.

"What's going on here?" she said as she ran down the hall. As Judy approached Caitlin's room, Will shouted with all of his might, praying that he would be heard above the rock music and alarms.

"Judy! Don't come in here alone! Get Major West. Get Mom and Dad. Get help! Fast!"

Will hoped that the fear in his voice would make Judy realize that this was no joke. Something terrible was happening in the cargo bay! If he was lucky, Judy would send out an emergency signal over her remote control. That way everyone aboard the ship could register her signal. And once the crew received the emergency signal, they would drop what they were doing to come to the location indicated.

Will could feel Caitlin's hot, fiery breath closing in on his back. He leaped out of the way just as she was going to lower the hard metal onto his head. He bent down and grabbed a piece of Robot's right arm.

"Sorry, buddy," Will told Robot. Then he swung the arm right at Caitlin's red eyes. But the alien jumped up and took a large bite out of the robotic arm, like a trained seal leaping up to grab a fish from its trainer.

"Thanks for the treat," she said sarcastically, pouncing on Will. Caitlin held Will tight against the ground as she prepared to lower the fatal blow.

"Freeze!"

Will was shocked — and relieved — as Major West's voice boomed across the room, surprising Caitlin. She jumped up, giving Will just enough time to move out from underneath her. Quickly, Will sprinted toward the door, practically colliding with his dad. Will darted out of the way, avoiding his father's laser gun, which was cocked and ready to shoot.

One look at his father's angry eyes and Will knew that his dad did not understand how much danger he was in.

"The emergency button is not a toy. . . ." Professor Robinson began. But as Carlos turned, Professor Robinson stopped his lecture dead.

Carlos's bloodred eyes glared at the professor. "No, the button is not a toy, Professor," he said. "And this is no game. We are going to take over this ship. And then we're going to take over each and every one of you."

13
The Battle

Will watched as his father stared into Carlos's burning eyes, then turned his head to look over at Will. As their eyes met, Will nodded slowly. He could see in his father's eyes that he regretted not trusting Will's instincts earlier. Will had a feeling his father would never make that mistake again. At least, not anytime soon.

Will watched with fascination as the Carlos-alien's face morphed back into human form. His eyes became soft and brown, and his tongue and teeth more normal.

Smart, Will thought. You have to admire that alien's perception. He's already figured out a bit of human psychology. He knows the grown-ups will never be able to destroy someone who looks like a child.

Will was right about the grown-ups. Already Professor Robinson was attempting to speak rationally to the alien.

"Okay, Carlos, relax. Tell us what you need, and we'll see what we can do, okay? You have no enemies here," Professor Robinson said calmly.

Will stared at his father. Was he really falling for Carlos's trap? This was not some teenager who could be grounded for misbehaving. This was a dangerous alien. But for some reason, his father could not get past the outer image Carlos had projected.

But Caitlin was another story. She wasn't playing any games. She wanted to kill the crew of the *Jupiter 2*. And she wanted to do it now. The second that Penny appeared, Caitlin jumped at her. Her eyes glowed even more viciously than before. She was like a wild animal on a hunt. Her nostrils flared. She opened her lips slightly and bared her razor-sharp teeth. Then she lunged toward Penny's neck and aimed for the teenager's jugular vein. One bite and Penny would be dead.

"Aaaahh!" Penny's screams filled the air.

From behind him, Will could hear the sounds of tiny footsteps. And those footsteps weren't human.

What now? Will wondered.

"Blawp! Blawp! Blawp!"

Suddenly, out of nowhere, Blawp appeared and leaped toward the Caitlin-monster. She bashed wildly into Caitlin's stomach. The alien doubled over in surprise and pain. Then Blawp jumped up onto Caitlin's shoulder and scratched at the skin on her neck and face. Caitlin reached up in pain and tried to brush the creature from her face. But Blawp just dug her claws in deeper.

Will stared at Caitlin's blood in surprise. The blood was red. Like human blood. Somehow Will had expected it to be green, or blue, or some sort of weird alien shade of magenta. Anything but red. No wonder Judy's equipment had registered the blood as human.

Caitlin was shocked but not conquered. She regained her bearings, stood tall, and took off after Penny once again. But Penny got away when her mom reached over and grabbed Caitlin by the arm. She yanked the arm backward and locked

68

it against the alien girl's back. Maureen held on tightly as Caitlin squirmed in her grip. But Caitlin was far stronger than your average eleven-year-old girl.

"Mom, watch out!" Penny shouted as Caitlin reached her arms up over her head and flipped Maureen across the room.

Penny watched anxiously as Judy raced to their mother's defense. Penny's big sister bent her fingers like claws and reached toward Caitlin's neck. Penny knew exactly what Judy was up to. Her big sister wasn't trying to injure the alien; she just wanted to subdue her. And the best way Judy knew to do that was to use the pads of her fingers to apply pressure to certain areas of the body. Caitlin's body seemed human enough.

"Judy, that won't work!" Will warned his sister. Will had already deduced that after hours of eating metal, Caitlin's body must have become harder than any human form Judy had ever met up with. Acupressure would not work on her. Caitlin stuck out her long forked tongue and hissed angrily.

Major West took out his ray gun and prepared to shoot. But Carlos snuck up behind the major and whacked him hard in the center of his back. Don's arm flew up, and the gun fell from his hand.

The gun landed with a loud crash on the floor of the cabin. Carlos reached out and grabbed for it. But Penny was quicker. She reached under Carlos's torso and snatched the gun away. Then Penny's eyes met Carlos's. She could not believe that he was truly as vicious as he seemed. She simply refused to accept that she could have been so easily fooled. Surely, deep down, Carlos cared about her and her family. Penny stared pleadingly into his brown eyes, hoping to silently convince him to stop this violence before someone got hurt.

Carlos stared back at Penny. But his eyes showed no mercy. Instead they once again morphed into the eyes of a horrifying creature. Penny was mesmerized by the red, fiery glow that returned to his pupils. As she stared into Carlos's eyes, she found herself unable to move. Will watched his sister with fear. Carlos was hypnotizing Penny into submission. Already, Carlos had bared his sharklike fangs. In a second, Penny would be killed! Will had to do something.

"Penny! Run!" Will shouted as he head-butted Carlos in the stomach.

The shift in Carlos's eyes and the sound of her brother's voice shocked Penny back into reality. She kicked at Carlos's knees, trying to knock him to the ground. Professor Robinson joined Penny in her battle and slammed Carlos in the shoulder blades, knocking him to the ground — if only for an instant. But that instant was just enough to allow Penny and Will the time to move out of harm's way. Penny ran through the door to the safety of her cabin. Will was about to follow when he saw Carlos delivering blows to Professor Robinson's chest and arms. Will froze in his tracks. He knew that his father could not fight the alien off for long. Carlos and Caitlin were not going to be beaten using traditional human battle techniques. Will looked over at his half-eaten Robot. These were not humans. These were wild metal-eating animals! Will had to save his family.

Major West joined Professor Robinson in his battle against Carlos. And that's when Will got an idea. He snuck out of the room and raced up to the bridge of the *Jupiter 2*. He had a plan for saving the crew.

This had better work, Will thought nervously as he approached the command chair. It's our only hope.

14
The Crew's Last Chance

"What are you doing up here?"

The cold, heartless voice ringing out from the bridge caught Will by surprise. He jumped up and hid quietly behind the open door. But after he caught his bearings, Will remembered that he knew that booming voice well.

"Dr. Smith, why are you up here?" Will asked as he moved away from the doorway.

Dr. Smith stood up from his hiding place but didn't answer. Up to something sneaky, as usual, Will thought.

Will moved quickly to the control panel and studied the buttons carefully. In spite of his scientific genius, he still had trouble figuring out all of the controls on the *Jupiter 2*. And if he pushed the wrong button . . .

Will didn't want to think about what could happen if he made a mistake. He had no choice but to try. Finally Will's eyes settled on a small black button located just to the left of the oxygen monitor.

"What are you doing?" Dr. Smith demanded.

Will ignored him. Instead he crossed his fingers, said a silent prayer, and pushed the small black button.

At first nothing happened. Will's hopes sank. That was their last chance. There was no way left to escape the monsters.

Then, suddenly, Will felt a rumbling beneath the bridge control panel. The ship rocked slightly from side to side. The lights blinked on and off as a surge of power rushed through the *Jupiter 2*.

"Now what have you done?" Dr. Smith barked angrily at Will.

. Will wasn't sure. But he acted as confident as he could. "Be quiet," he whispered to Dr. Smith. "Do you want them to know we're up here?"

Dr. Smith couldn't argue with that. He followed Will's glance and stared at the control panel. A red light began blinking furiously. Will ran over to the computer. Words raced across the screen. They read MAGNETIC SHIELDS IN PLACE.

Will jumped up in the air with his fist raised. "All right!" he declared.

"So the magnetic shields are in place," Dr. Smith said. "What does that mean?"

Will smiled and grabbed Dr. Smith by the arm. "That's just what we're about to find out," Will said as he dragged Dr. Smith off the bridge and down the corridor toward Caitlin's quarters.

"Now just be quiet, and maybe they won't notice us," Will warned Dr. Smith as they walked. "Let's hope all of the danger is over by now."

Dr. Smith didn't say a word.

As the two of them neared the cargo bay, Will could hear the *boom, boom, boom* of the bass line exploding from the musical broadcast system. As he came close to the doorway, he could also make out various voices. His parents were still shouting at the aliens. That was good. It meant they were still alive.

But there was one sound that truly frightened Will. Above the din, he could hear deep, throaty growls. Caitlin and Carlos were still alive, too, and still on the loose.

"Mom! Dad! Are you all . . ." Will turned the corner into the room and stopped in the middle of his sentence. His parents were obviously all right. In fact, everyone was all right. Everyone, that is, except for Carlos and Caitlin. They weren't on the loose anymore. They were being held prisoner in a magnetic trap. The animallike noises Will had heard in the corridor were the sounds of Caitlin and Carlos growling and struggling to free themselves. But they weren't going to be able to wrest themselves from this trap. Will had seen to that.

"Will! Where have you been? Are you all right?" his mother exclaimed as Will entered the room. "Did you do this?" she asked, pointing to Carlos and Caitlin. The two aliens were held tight against the wall, suspended in midair.

"I'm fine, Mom," Will answered. Then he flicked on his transmitter and paged Penny back to the cargo bay.

"It's all right. Everyone's safe. You can come back now," he told her through his pager.

Will could hear his sister's footsteps coming down the hall. When Penny reached the door she peered in cautiously and entered nervously. Her eyes registered surprise as she saw Carlos and Caitlin dangling helplessly from the wall.

"Who did that? And how?" Penny asked.

Will laughed. "Me. And it was simple," he said proudly. "I told you there was something weird about these two. And one of the weirdest things is that they are not human."

"Obviously," Penny answered, rolling her eyes. "Now stop gloating and start explaining how you got them to stick to the wall."

Will began to explain, "Caitlin told me that she needed

73

metal to maintain her iron level. And I knew that she and Carlos had been eating Robot in order to survive." Will winced as he looked down at his injured friend. "I figured that with all that metal inside of them, they would stick to magnets. So, I went up on the deck and put the magnetic shields in place. It's the *Jupiter 2*'s magnetic shields that are holding Carlos and Caitlin against the walls now."

Professor Robinson put his arm around Will. "Good job, son," he said simply.

"I guess I owe you a big apology, little bro," Penny said. "You warned me, but I didn't believe you."

Will grinned. An apology from Penny. A real apology with no crossed fingers. Now that was something for the history books!

"Ahem." Dr. Smith cleared his throat. "I hate to interrupt this precious little scene, but I'd like to know just what you plan to do with these prisoners, Professor Robinson."

15
Disclosure

W ill looked pointedly at his father. What *was* he going to
do with Caitlin and Carlos?

"Well, that depends," Professor Robinson said slowly.

"Depends!" Dr. Smith barked. "Depends on what?"

"It depends on what these two have to say for themselves.
This is still a United States ship, Smith," Professor Robinson
declared. "And we can't just convict people without allowing
them to defend themselves."

Professor Robinson walked toward the wall where Caitlin
and Carlos were being held prisoner. Will watched as his father stood a safe distance away and avoided their burning red
eyes. "Do you have anything to say?" he asked the aliens
pointedly.

Suddenly, the two became subdued. They stopped struggling and the fire in their eyes dulled to a low red. They looked
nervously at each other, unsure of what to do next. Finally,
Caitlin began to speak.

"We come from a planet in a galaxy far from your Earth,"
she began slowly. "Our planet had enough iron and metal in its
surface to feed a thousand generations. But our people became

greedy. We didn't treat the planet with respect, and before long many of our food sources became contaminated. What few healthy metals were still within the planet's surface were disappearing at an alarming rate. We knew we didn't have long to survive as a species. We had to do something to preserve our people and our heritage."

Will and Penny glanced knowingly at one another. It was amazing just how much Caitlin's and Carlos's story sounded like their own.

"We had to get off the planet and find a new home — one that would support our people's need for iron and other metals. But to do that we would have to build a very sophisticated space vehicle — one that was capable of sustaining us for as long as it would take to find such a planet. And we had no idea how long that would be," Caitlin continued.

"But a ship like that would require an enormous amount of metal," Penny interrupted.

"Exactly," Caitlin replied. "Metal that our people needed for food. We had already ingested the metal from almost all of our space vehicles. There was only one left in working order. And that could hold only thirteen people and enough food to last three months. Our only hope was to find a safe planet quickly. But that was not to be. It has been almost twenty years since we left our planet, I assume the rest of our people have died of starvation by now."

The crew of the *Jupiter 2* was silent. They thought how frightening it must be to know that you have no home planet to return to.

"Wait a minute. Something doesn't make sense," Major West interjected. "If the ship could only carry food for three months, how is it you have survived twenty years?"

Carlos continued Caitlin's story. "We floated with our comrades for a long while. At one point we came near to your home galaxy. And that's when we began getting signals from a ship called the *Taurus*. Perhaps you've heard of it."

Will nodded. Everyone had heard of the *Taurus*. It was one of the first things Earth kids studied in history class. The *Taurus* had been the subject of lots of movies, books, and even a live stage show. One of the largest space stations ever built, the *Taurus* had been launched more than twenty years ago. The space station was manned by three families who were prepared to live for four years as a community in space. But the *Taurus* had disappeared without a trace before it reached its destination. It was assumed everyone on board had died in some sort of undetectable explosion.

Will was amazed. Wait until he told his history teacher this one! Could all the history books be wrong? Was it possible the crew of the *Taurus* had somehow survived?

"We stormed the ship and took it over. We forced the crew of the *Taurus* to steer the space station away from your galaxy, hoping that the families on board would help us locate a new home planet. But that was not to be — not because the crew of the *Taurus* wasn't helpful, but because finding such a planet was taking longer than expected. And we needed food to survive. We soon discovered that there was only one way we could live on board the *Taurus*. We would have to invade human bodies. That way we could slow our metabolism to a human rate, and we would be able to survive on metal sources from the ship for a longer period of time. So that's what we did."

"Then where are the other members of your mission?" Major West demanded.

"Dead," Caitlin said simply. "Their bodies could not adjust to their human forms. But somehow ours did. We were able to

77

adjust to the human structure almost entirely, which is why we were able to fool Judy's medical equipment. Only the iron content in our human blood could be detected by her machinery. The rest of our body parts could be kept hidden behind the human features."

Will listened closely. Now he had the solution to the problem with the navigational systems. Obviously the high iron content in Carlos's and Caitlin's bodies had been throwing off the magnetic equipment. And the fear of rusting had kept Carlos and Caitlin from the showers. It was all coming together now.

Will knew Judy was fascinated with Carlos's and Caitlin's physical makeup. From a professional point of view, it was something she had never experienced. "If you've been in a human form for twenty years, why haven't you aged?" she asked.

"We were able to use certain minerals in our diet to continuously regenerate the human cells in our host bodies," Carlos explained. "Nothing in our human form has ever deteriorated or aged. However, we have continued to mature in our natural form. We are both well into our adult states now.

"We were in danger of dying from starvation when we discovered your ship on the radar," Carlos continued. "We had eaten so much of the *Taurus* that it was about to self-destruct. In fact, we barely had enough time to get into the probe ship before the *Taurus* blew up."

"We planned to travel along with the *Jupiter 2* until we could find a suitable planet upon which to mate and begin a new civilization," Caitlin added.

"In other words, you'd planned to kill us all, the way you killed the crew of the *Taurus*," Dr. Smith remarked.

"No, Dr. Smith. Killing you would not have served our purpose," Carlos said. His eyes had a sudden flash of red fiery heat

78

before cooling down to brown again. "You see, we had to learn how to run your ship. The only people we could learn that from was you. That is why we created the story about losing our family. We knew that would increase sympathy for us and make you less suspicious. Your sympathy ensured that you would include us in conversations that involved crucial information."

Will nodded. He had to admit, these aliens were smart. Luckily they weren't smarter than he was. He'd suspected them almost from the start.

"So why try to kill us now?" Will asked.

Carlos stared at Will. "You'd caught on to us, Will. Besides, we'd hoped to begin the reproduction process quite soon. Our offspring would have needed host bodies. If we had not reached a suitable planet by then, well, yes, we would have had to invade your bodies, in effect killing you. Our survival instincts are strong."

"Obviously," Will said.

"You two have just admitted to attempted murder," Dr. Smith said. "Professor Robinson, isn't that crime punishable by death?"

Major West stared Dr. Smith straight in the eye. "If it is, Smith, then you should die first. Don't forget you've attempted murder, too."

Dr. Smith gulped, moved slowly to the corner of the room, and shut his mouth.

"Relax, Smith," Professor Robinson said. "No one is going to be killed on board this ship. These are the last two remaining members of their species. And as I have told you many times, this mission has always been about the preservation of life, not the destruction of it."

"I'm behind you one hundred percent — in theory, John,"

Maureen said gently. "But my survival instincts are as strong as theirs. And these two not only tried to kill us, they tried to kill our children. *Our* immortality. And I don't know if this explanation isn't just some new game plan of theirs. If we let them loose, there's no telling what they'll do!"

Her mother's words took Penny by surprise. Usually her mother was incredibly nonviolent. It wasn't like her to suggest killing the last surviving members of an entire race. But of course, this was an incredibly explosive situation. These aliens had shown extremely violent tendencies. And that seemed to be bringing out the violent tendencies in others. Penny couldn't argue with her mother's feelings.

Apparently neither could Major West. "I hate to agree with Smith, but even if we could help these creatures, we couldn't guarantee that they wouldn't kill again. Any species they might meet up with has the same right to survive as they do."

Will's eyes met his father's. He could tell that the Professor was in the midst of a moral dilemma. "Well, there's no sense discussing this here," Will's father said finally. "I suggest we move this conversation to the bridge."

16
Escape

The crew of the *Jupiter 2* followed Professor Robinson to the bridge. Will looked at his family. They seemed worn-out, both physically and emotionally.

"I simply cannot put those two to death," Professor Robinson said. "I cannot look in their eyes and condemn them."

"But those are not *their* eyes, John," Maureen said solemnly. "Those are the eyes of two innocent children. Two kids who they killed. Two kids who might have been *our* kids — had Will not been able to stop them."

Will felt a shiver go up and down his spine. "They aren't really humans, Dad. If we could strip away their bodies you would see their true form. Then it would probably be an easier decision for you to make."

"EEEAAWWWW!"

Suddenly a bloodcurdling scream came from the direction of Carlos's and Caitlin's quarters. Could they have broken free? Will spun around and, sure enough, the two aliens were coming toward the bridge.

"AAAIWWW!" A decidedly nonhuman voice shot through

81

the body of the alien who had disguised itself as Caitlin. Its bloodred eyes searched anxiously for a victim.

The other alien bared its metal fangs hungrily. The aliens must have used sheer desperation to gather enough strength to break free of their magnetic prison.

Dr. Smith rose from his chair and dove for the console. Before Will could stop him, the doctor reached for the button that controlled the magnetic shields.

"Nooo!!!!" Will cried out. But it was too late. The shields rose to their highest position. Every metal object on the bridge flew straight to the walls. Suddenly, Will felt a powerful gust of air. The full strength of the magnetic shields had forced a hole in the exterior of the *Jupiter 2*. The Robinsons, Major West, and Dr. Smith took the emergency precautions they had trained for and held tight to the stationary objects in the room.

But the alien monsters weren't so lucky. The metal in their body was immediately attracted to the now-exposed magnetic shields. Their bodies sailed across the room. They were helpless. Will and Penny watched in shock as Caitlin and Carlos were sucked out of the *Jupiter 2* and into the darkness of space.

Will breathed a sigh of relief. A tear dripped down Penny's cheek. They both knew the truth. The aliens' human forms could not survive the airlessness of space without oxygen masks.

Carlos and Caitlin would kill no more.

The crew of the *Jupiter 2* was silent for a second. Then Major West jumped to attention. He cautiously made his way over to the console. Instantly he put up a protective shield to close the hole in the ship. Then he lowered the magnetic shields.

* * *

It took about two days for Major West and Professor Robinson to permanently correct the puncture in the ship's outer hull. When the job was finally completed, Professor Robinson gave the order to leave the moon's surface. "Prepare for take-off," he announced. "Major West, choose your direction."

Major West set the navigational controls for a direction the group had never gone in before. Then he waited for Professor Robinson's countdown. At the word "one," the *Jupiter 2* set off on its new course.

As soon as the ship had steadied, everyone was able to return to their cabins. But Penny and Will stayed on the bridge, staring out the main viewport into space.

"Will, I really thought Carlos was human," Penny confided. "But it was all just a fantasy."

"More like a nightmare," Will replied with a shudder.

"Maybe," Penny said. "But for awhile it was nice to have a friend. What if this whole idea of being able to return to Earth is a fantasy, too? What if we're the only humans we'll ever see again?"

Will shook his head, He refused to allow himself to believe that. "Look, Pen, you found a friend in this solar system. Maybe he wasn't a real friend, but for a time you thought you had one. And that was a good time. Maybe there's another friend in the next solar system. A real friend. And maybe this time we really are heading home. . . ."

"Get this beast away from me!" Dr. Smith's voice echoed through the corridors, interrupting Will and Penny's conversation.

"Blawp! Blawp! Blawp!"

Will started to laugh as Dr. Smith approached the bridge. Once again, Blawp was chasing him wildly.

"Nice to see things are back to normal," Penny whispered to Will.

Normal? Will thought as he watched the scaly lizard monkey chase a homocidal doctor. Well, he thought, as normal as things can be when you're lost in space.